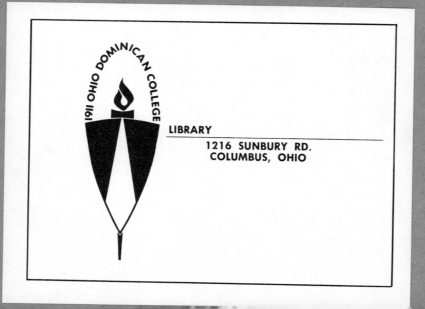

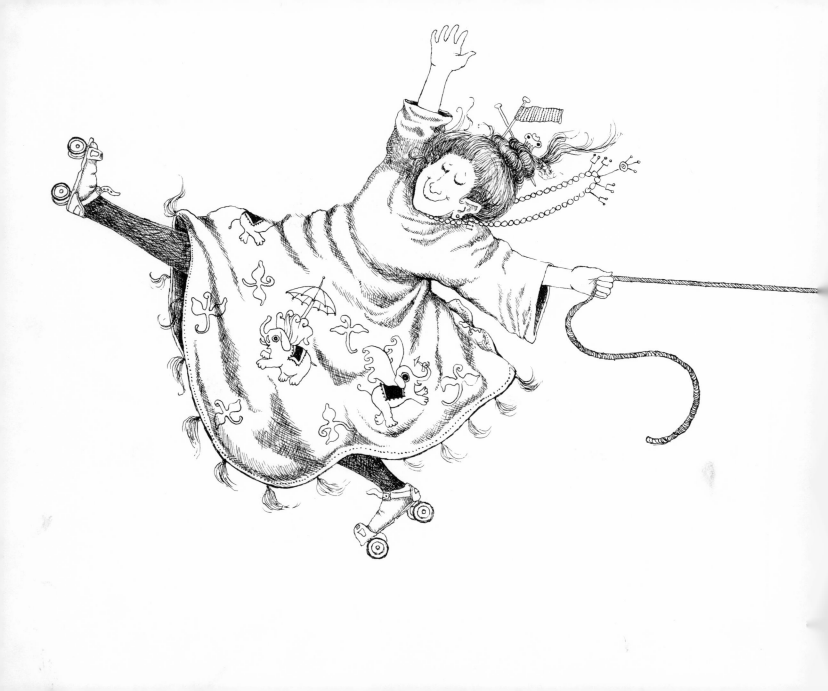

Kevin's Grandma

by

Barbara Williams

illustrated by Kay Chorao

E. P. Dutton & Co., Inc. / New York

Library of Congress Cataloging in Publication Data

Williams, Barbara   Kevin's grandma

SUMMARY: Kevin's friend has a grandma who plays
checkers and makes caramel popcorn balls, but Kevin's
grandma gives judo lessons, goes skydiving, and does lots
of other un-grandmotherly things.

[1. Grandparents — Fiction]   I. Chorao, Kay, illus.
II. Title.
PZ7.W65587Ke   [E]   74-23713   ISBN 0-525-33115-8

Published simultaneously in Canada by Clarke,
Irwin & Company Limited, Toronto and Vancouver

Designed by Riki Levinson
Printed in the U.S.A.   First Edition
10 9 8 7 6 5 4 3 2 1

To Gil, who never lies—
just makes the truth more interesting

I tell Kevin about my grandma. When I am sick she comes to see me in her blue station wagon and brings presents like crayons and coloring books and cartons of ice cream.

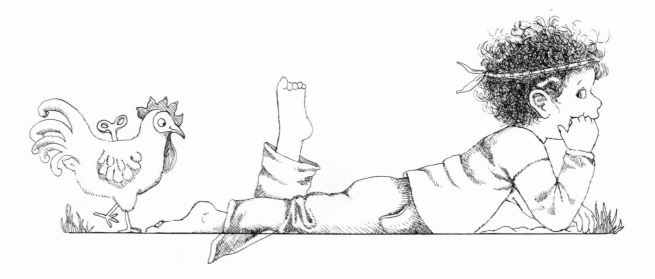

Then Kevin tells me about his grandma. When Kevin is
sick she brings him things like *Mad* magazine and homemade
peanut-butter soup, which she delivers on her Honda 90.

I like to sleep at my grandma's house when my parents
go out of town. We play checkers and drink root beer and
sometimes stay up as late as ten-thirty.

Kevin likes to sleep at his grandma's house, too. They arm-wrestle and do yoga exercises and send out for pizza at midnight.

Sometimes I help my grandma work. We put on white aprons
to shell peas or make caramel popcorn balls.

Sometimes Kevin helps his grandma work. They put on
bib overalls to fix her Honda chain or hammer the shingles
on her roof.

I take piano lessons from my grandma. After each recital she takes all the kids to the ice cream parlor for a sundae or a malted.

Kevin takes judo lessons from his grandma. Afterwards they go to the health-food bar and drink tiger's milk.

My grandma belongs to a bridge club and a garden club and a music club. Last winter her music club put on a Christmas program for the children in the hospital.

Kevin's grandma belongs to a karate club and a scuba-diver's club and a mountain-climbing club. Last winter her mountain-climbing club spent Christmas on the top of the Grand Tetons.

On my birthday my grandma takes me out to lunch. Then we go shopping and she buys me any toy I want.

On Kevin's birthday his grandma takes him in an airplane.
He watches from the window while she goes skydiving.

My grandma has a scrapbook showing all the things she used to do. She was the lead in her junior high school play.

Kevin's grandma used to work in a circus. She has a scrapbook with pictures showing how she could ride a unicycle on a tight rope and swing from a trapeze by her teeth and put her head in a lion's mouth.

Once my grandma took me on a trip to Florida. We went
in her air-conditioned blue station wagon and stopped over-
night in a motel.

Once Kevin's grandma took him on a trip to California.
They rode in twenty-seven different cars and trucks and
slept in haystacks and barns and in a floating all-night
monster movie in the middle of Lake Tahoe.

I'm not sure I believe everything about Kevin's grandma.

Whoever heard of peanut-butter soup?

BARBARA WILLIAMS is the author of several children's books, including *Albert's Toothache,* illustrated by Kay Chorao. Mrs. Williams can't remember a time when she didn't consider herself a writer. Her children often tease her about the notebooks she lugs around, jotting down ideas for stories. Mrs. Williams and her family live in Salt Lake City, Utah.

KAY CHORAO grew up in Cleveland, Ohio, and was graduated from Wheaton College in Massachusetts. She went to London for graduate study at the Chelsea School of Art. Along with her illustrations for *Albert's Toothache* and other books, she is the author-illustrator of *The Repair of Uncle Toe.*

The display type was set in Bertha and the text in Vladimir. The line art was prepared with pen and ink and the book was printed by offset at Halliday Lithographers.

101176

DATE DUE

J
W
Williams, Barbara
  Kevin's grandma.

Ohio Dominican College Library
1216 Sunbury Road
Columbus, Ohio 43219

DEMCO